A Home for Panda

by Ann Whitehead Nagda

Illustrated by Jim Effler

To Kirit — A.W.N.

For my wife, Debbie, and daughters, Jenna and Ariana — J.E.

Published by Soundprints Division of Trudy Corporation, Norwalk, Connecticut.

Book design: Marcin D. Pilchowski
Editor: Laura Gates Galvin
Editorial assistance: Chelsea Shriver

First Edition 2003
10 9 8 7 6 5 4 3 2 1
Printed in China

Acknowledgments:
  Our very special thanks to the staff of the National Zoological Park in Washington DC, especially Lisa Stevens, for their review and guidance.

Library of Congress Cataloging-in-Publication Data is on file with the publisher and the Library of Congress.

A Home for Panda

by Ann Whitehead Nagda

Illustrated by Jim Effler

Soundprints

Where Children Discover...

In a bamboo thicket high in the mountains of China, all is quiet except for the pitter-patter of autumn rain. The fat drops slide off the bamboo leaves and drip onto the fur of a sleeping panda.

Panda is two years old. He left his mother several months ago and now he must find his own home.

Waking from his nap, Panda yawns and reaches for a bamboo stem. But the stem in front of him suddenly disappears into the ground.

A bamboo rat has stolen it! With strong, sharp teeth, the rat cut the stem and pulled it into an underground tunnel. There, the rat nibbles the bamboo.

Panda is hungry! He moves to another bamboo patch. Just as he sits down, a huge angry panda runs at him. *Roar!* She does not want to share her home with him! She slaps at him with her paw. Panda turns his head away and covers his eyes with his paws to show that he does not want to fight. He moans and moves away. The angry panda huffs and walks back to her baby in a hollow tree.

Panda crosses a stream and finds more bamboo, but all the leaves and stalks are brown and brittle. He chews on a stem, but he does not feel full. Panda must find tender green bamboo to eat.

Panda lumbers down the mountain and crosses into a forest where thick stalks of bamboo grow. He grabs a mouthful of bamboo leaves.

As Panda rests against an oak tree, acorn shells drop beside him. A moon bear stands in the tree. The bear peels acorns with its teeth and eats the nut kernels. Looking down, the moon bear growls and Panda scrambles away. He is still very hungry.

Late at night, Panda wanders by a stone house in a village. Yummy smells come from inside the kitchen. Panda pushes open the door and finds a pot of leftover rice and pork next to the stove.

Crash! Panda knocks over the pot. A farmer and his wife wake up and chase Panda away, yelling and waving blankets.

The next morning, Panda finds some steamed bread left near the river. As Panda starts to eat the bread, he hears barking. A pack of wild dogs races toward him. He looks around for an escape. There are no trees for him to climb. He runs to the river and plunges into the ice-cold water. He swims frantically, but the river carries him downstream.

Panda climbs out on the opposite bank and shakes himself dry. He hurries uphill to a forest of birch trees. Now safe, he stops to drink from a stream.

Suddenly, Panda is startled by the sound of branches snapping and crashing. Above him, long-haired golden monkeys leap from tree to tree.

18

Snow begins to fall. Panda is still hungry. He must find more bamboo to eat soon! He reaches the edge of another forest. Once again, the bamboo in this forest is dry and brittle. When he stops to eat a clump of blackberries, he frightens two pheasants who dart away and hide under a bush.

Panda shuffles on, wandering for miles without finding anything to eat. He passes a large bull munching on tender leaves.

After hours of plodding through the deepening snow, Panda stops to gnaw on some tree bark. Below him lies a valley.

Large snowflakes swirl around as Panda
heads downhill. He finds a patch of bamboo
growing beneath the tree branches.

A bamboo rat stares at him with beady
eyes. Pulling a bamboo stem into its burrow,
the rat disappears underground.

Panda sits down and stuffs tender leaves
into his mouth. He fills his empty stomach.
Finally, for the first time in days, Panda is full.
He falls asleep.

Just before dawn, Panda happily munches on more of the tasty bamboo. By daybreak, he is thirsty. He slides down the snowy hill on his stomach. He hears the gurgling of a mountain stream and climbs over boulders to drink the icy water. Downstream, he finds more bamboo! Lying on a bed of dry fir tree needles, he pulls bamboo stems to his mouth and eats and eats.

Finally Panda has a place to call home!

THE GIANT PANDA LIVES IN CHINA

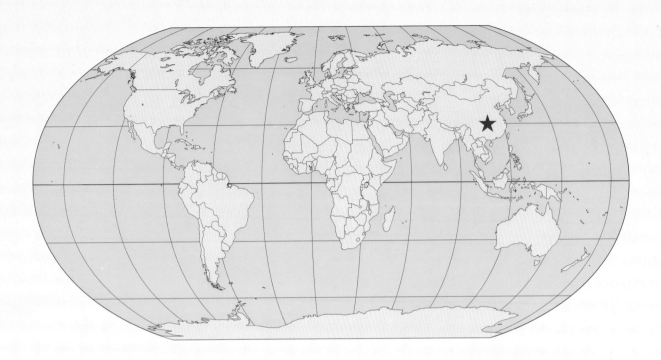

ABOUT THE GIANT PANDA

The striking black and white markings of the giant panda make it one of the most recognizable animals in the world. However, giant pandas are not really that giant! They range in size from 5 to 6 feet tall, and weigh from 190 to 275 pounds. At birth, giant pandas only weigh about 4 ounces.

Even though bamboo makes up about 95% of a panda's diet, giant pandas will also eat fish, vines, mushrooms and sometimes even small rodents. Because bamboo remains green and edible all year long, giant pandas do not need to hibernate.

Giant pandas have roamed the bamboo forests of Asia for over one million years.